My Little Book of Greatness

My Little Book

of

Greatness

Lisa Colman-Smith

First hardcover edition 2023

Book design by Lisa Colman-Smith

Illustrator: Copper Fermina

Reference to Novak Djokovic taken from his 2019 Wimbledon winners interview Novak Djokovic Wimbledon 2019 Winner's Speech

978-1-80541-084-3 (hardcover)
978-1-80227-705-0 (ebook)

In loving memory of Imogen Tothill
who embodied all of the principles
contained in this book

CONTENTS

ACKNOWLEDGEMENTS

I strongly believe that the emotional wellbeing of our children is just as important as their physical wellbeing and with mental health issues on the rise, I wanted to create something special, that will help to build resilience, perspective and above all, hope for our future generations.

I would like to thank my beautiful family for their support and inspiration during this process and to my amazing friends, who have helped me across the finish line. I love you all.

This book is dedicated in loving memory of Imogen Tothill, who embodied all of the principles within this book and more. Your beautiful energy will continue to make a difference in this world for many years to come.

It is my dream that this book finds its way into the hands of millions of children around the world, allowing us to raise a generation that know, without question, that their potential holds no limits.

With only love

Lisa xx

Ava's Awesome Glasses

Ava is a friendly child, loving, warm and kind.
Qualities that sometimes seem a little hard to find.
So, on beginning her adventure and starting at her school,
She realised sometimes kids could be a little cruel.
Believing that the world was the most beautiful place,
It was hard for her to see this was not always the case.

So, on the journey to school, on the hardest of her days,
Her mother started teaching her some very curious ways,
To focus all her thoughts, away from all the bad
And to look around her everywhere for reasons to be glad.

She said, "Ava, as you start to grow, you'll soon begin to know,

That when you focus on your problems, you will surely make them grow.

So, I have some glasses here for you that no one else can see,

That will make everything you look at, as good as it can be.

A wise man said to me one day, and at first it seemed so strange,

That if you change the way you look at things, the things you look at change."

Now Ava wears her glasses everywhere she goes.
She sees the good in everyone from their head down to
their toes.
So, try yours on for size right now and adjust your point
of view,
Then every day is sure to be so awesome, just like you!

THE BUBBLE OF RESILIENCE

From the outside world looking in, Ava seemed to shine,
And to all the friends who knew her well, she appeared
to be just fine.

But sometimes she's not fine at all and the glasses just
won't do,
So her mother showed her one more trick she knew
would help her through.

She said, "When you wake up each day, imagine there's a bubble

That's wrapped up all around you to protect you from your trouble."
The bubble is completely yours, to design just how you like. You can have it pink or blue or green, even sparkly or striped. Your bubble is there to shield you whenever life gets tough.
Sticks and stones cannot get through and words will bounce right off.

You see everything is energy; yes, that's even you!
And it's important to protect yours in everything you do.

It's hard to believe when explained this way how simple this can be,
But try yours on for size right now and soon you too will see.

The resilience bubble is hard to pop,
So wear yours now with pride
And soon you will trust it works for you.
Believe me, I know, I've tried.

DREAM BIG

When Ava was a little girl, she was told to sit up straight.
They told her almost every day that her daydreaming could wait.
But if you knew the power your dreams could truly hold,
You would dream big dreams the whole day long and watch as they unfold.

Dream of being an astronaut and flying off to space,
Winning the Champions League or coming first in a major race.
Dancing on a great big stage or whatever fills your heart.
Just close your eyes and picture it now, it's the perfect place to start.

Think of Novak Djokovic, who dreamed he'd one day be,
Champion of Wimbledon for all the world to see.
He made himself a trophy, as though he always knew, that
he'd be standing on Centre Court, on grass he'd one day
chew.

Take all the greats in history and you'll see they share one
thing.
It's pure determination and trust in what dreams can bring.

So, close your eyes and dream your dream, be bold and free from fear.
Be sure to feel the way you'd feel if your dream was already here.

For if you can see it in your heart and mind, you can hold it in your hand.
The trick is to see it crystal clear, as though it's happening where you stand.
It's hard to put a timescale on when your dreams come true,
But trust that if you do it right, I know they always do.

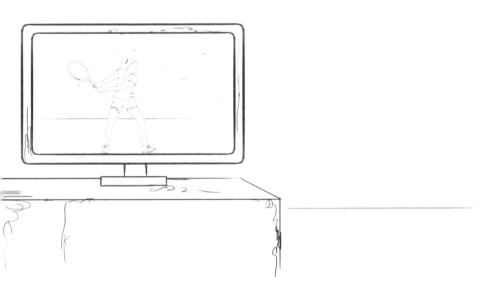

Life Is a Magnificent Magnet

Life's a magnificent magnet you carry on your back
And everything you put out there is sure to come right back.
So, choose your words more carefully and your thoughts and feelings too.
Stay positive and grateful in everything you do.

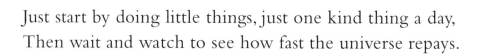

Just start by doing little things, just one kind thing a day,
Then wait and watch to see how fast the universe repays.

Positivity

Kindness

Care

It's called the law of attraction and it operates worldwide,
So that every act of kindness is impossible to hide.
You may not yet have heard of it but it's as real as me and you
And it's a pretty cool phenomena that reflects in all you do.

15

So, put your magnet to the test and show it to be true,
By keeping an eye on all the things that are heading straight for you.
By being what you want others to be and reflecting what you desire,
Becoming what you respect in me and mirroring what you admire.

Just start by telling the universe exactly what you want,
And you'll start to see a change take place; come tell me
if you don't.
So, remember what I have told you and what many have
also taught,
That all that you will ever be is a result of what you
thought.

There's No Such Thing As Failure

If at first you don't succeed, try and try again

I bet you've heard this many times, it comes from way back when.

But does anybody really see the importance of not quitting?

Because you never know just how close to victory you could be sitting.

I'd love sit and tell you that you are always going to win,
But even superheroes fail the first time they begin.
So, get up off your knees, my child, and wipe away your tears,
'Cos the only thing that's stopping you is self-belief and fears.

Look at Henry Ford, who made the first automobile,
It took him several times before his vision became real.
What do you think would have happened if he'd given up first time?
You'd be going to school by horse and cart; it would have changed the course of time.

Or think about the Wright brothers' dream to fly across the land.

A feat of engineering most find hard to understand.

But if they gave up on their first attempt, we may never have got to see,

The far-off distant shores we dream we'd one day love to be.

So, the moral of this story is to never give up hope,
Because there's no such thing as failure, just opportunities
for growth.

CHANGE THOSE WORN-OUT SHOES

Imagine that your comfort zone is like your favourite shoe,
You wear it everywhere you go 'cos it feels good to you.
It may have seen much better days, but you really just don't care,
You just can't imagine a better shoe to take you anywhere.

But did you know the comfy choice is not always the best,
Sometimes it's more important to put life to the test.
You see, some roads we have to take are not the easiest to travel,
So it's important to select a shoe that helps you win the battle.
It may not fit you perfectly or even look the best,
But it will take you where you need to go and guide you through each test.

Most people are afraid to put their comfort zone aside,
'Cos it's a warm and cosy place to be; it's the perfect place
to hide.
So, take a leap of faith and change those worn-out shoes,
my dear,
Because everything you dream to be is on the other side
of fear.

YOUR JOURNEY

Sadly, people spend their lives dwelling on the past,
Or worrying about a future that has not yet come to pass.
By doing this, I have to say, you will surely miss
The power in this moment now: the beauty and the bliss.

It's everywhere around you from the mountains to the trees,
You can witness it in nature most, in the bird song and the bees.
So, close your eyes, take a breath and let yourself just be,
Because the most important thing in life is the here and now, you'll see.

It can help you in so many ways, from truly listening
To focusing more clearly on what you've been envisioning.
By staying in this moment, your woes you will surmount,
'Cos while the destination's an important one, it's the
journey that really counts.

DIVERSITY

When you enter Ava's classroom, it's pretty clear to see,
That at first glance there's no one else that looks like you
or me.
Everyone has differences, some subtle and some bold.
It's what makes the world a better place, if the truth be
told.

Whether your difference is religion, your heritage or race,
The clothes you wear, who you love, or the adversities
you face.
Just know that, in the end, there's only one thing that's in
fashion.
It's love and lots of kindness, loyalty and compassion.

See, everybody's light is bright, however it may shine,
So be yourself and know that it will always be just fine.
If people don't accept you, that's all on them, not you.
It's fine for you to be yourself, so just stay true to being
you.

So, shine your light far and bright in whatever way you know,
Or we may never get to see just how far you have to go.
You have a special gift to share that the world would love to see,
So sing it loud and sing it proud and let yourself be free.

Your Tribe Is Your Vibe

Sometimes we feel the pressure to follow with the crowd,
Even when the things they do don't make us feel too proud.
But I am here to tell you now, that things don't have to be this way,
So listen very carefully to what I have to say.

It's easier to follow those you think arc cool,
Especially when you think it helps you fit in at your school.
But don't you know it's cooler to follow your own path
And surround yourself with people who are good and make you laugh.

So, make the right decisions, even when they're not the norm,
And stand up for the underdog when surrounded by a storm.
Think about the consequences of everything you do
Because who you spend your time with, becomes who you are too.

Please know it's not who's beautiful, it's who they are inside,
So if someone makes you feel good, be sure you've found your tribe.

HAPPINESS IS INSIDE OF YOU

Ava is a lucky girl who likes to have nice things.
She sees them all around her and thinks happiness they bring.
"I want a concert ticket, I want a picture for my room.
I want the latest Ariana Grande Cloud perfume.
I want an iPhone 13 Pro, the one I've got's no good.
My friends already have it, so I really think I should.

No, actually, Mum, scrap all those things, I really want a puppy.
My life would be complete for sure; that would really make me happy."

"Ava, now I hope you know you have really got it wrong,
Acquiring all those things today won't make you happy for long.
You see, all you need is love, they say, and nothing can be more true,
But the most important thing to love, by far, is always you.

That's how you find happiness and I hope one day you'll see
That loving yourself for who you are, really is the key.
You may not be rich and famous or wear expensive clothes,
But you'll be full of joy and happiness and my, that really shows."

EMOTIONS ARE YOUR GUIDE

Have you ever had a feeling when you lie in bed at night
That the decisions that you made today may just not be
quite right?
Some call it intuition, a gut feeling or a hunch
And it can be a simple choice of who you sat next to for
lunch.

It's hard to know, sometimes in life, what the right choice is to make,
So we spend a lot of time deciding which path we should take.
But we have an inner guidance that some people just ignore
And if you listen very closely, you may hear it try to roar.

You can feel it in the words you say and in the actions that you take
By doing the things you love to do or in the little things you make.
Emotions are your GPS that help you stay on track,
If some things don't feel good to you, be sure to turn right back.

So, when you can't find your direction and don't know which way to go,
Just take a look inside of you because your emotions always know.

COMPARISON IS A THIEF

Have I told you of the villain who steals away your joy?
I am pretty sure he visits every girl and every boy.
His name's comparison and he's a tricky one to spot.
He visits when you're with your friends or on a trip down
to the shop.

Comparison is hard to stop, so most people let him in.
He makes you feel unhappy watching other people win.
But I have found a way to keep this pesky villain far away
And it's to focus on how much I've grown, each and every
day.

It's natural to compare yourself to where other people stand.

You may see the things that others have and want them in your hand.

But trust me when I say that if you live your life this way,

You will find it hard to value all the gifts that come your way.

Now, please don't get me wrong, 'cos it's the hardest thing to stop,
But you will never know how hard they've worked to get to where they've got
Or the trials and tribulations they've faced along the way,
And the sorrow that they feel inside and may never get to say.
So, next time you bump into him, be sure to turn away,
Thank him for his time and wave him kindly on his way.
From now on, you just need to know that everything is fair
For there's enough abundance in the world for all of us to share.

46

Lightning Source UK Ltd.
Milton Keynes UK
UKHW051322220223
417163UK00010B/8

9 781805 410843